Two Little Farmers in One Wooden Shoe

Patricia McLaughlin

ISBN: Softcover   978-1-5245-0535-6
       Hardcover   978-1-5245-0536-3
       EBook   978-1-5245-0534-9

Print information available on the last page

Rev. date: 06/02/2016

To order additional copies of this book, contact:
Xlibris
1-888-795-4274
www.Xlibris.com
Orders@Xlibris.com

Jack and Maggie, so I've been told
Lived far away on Peppermint Road.

They lived on a farm way up on a hill
Just down the road from an old paper mill.

One sunny day Maggie said to Jack,
"Let's put all our clothes into one big sack

We'll go far away; see all new things
And bring back treasures like diamond rings.

We'll sail across the mighty ocean so blue,
We'll both fit inside a small wooden shoe.

It will be fun, Jack, you wait and see
We'll have so much fun, just you and me"

Now Jack wasn't sure this idea was so bright,
He just wasn't certain that Maggie was right

After all he decided can a shoe really float?
I've never seen one that was used as a boat!

But Jack was so bored with that farm on the hill
He thought that a trip might give him a thrill.

As Jack turned to Maggie he politely did say,
"Will we go on this new adventure today?

I'll pack us a lunch to fill both our bellies
I'll make us a dozen P.B.s and Jellies.

Then, I'll put in some pears and some apples too
I sure hope it will fit into that wooden shoe.

So, both of these two set out that fine day
Traveling over the land right to Bubble Gum Bay.

They boarded that shoe taking all of their wares,
All those P.B.s and Jellies and apples and pears.

They put up the sails; the wind blew them along
Just Maggie and Jack singing old sailor songs.

It wasn't too long 'til a storm came about
The wind was so loud it caused Maggie to shout.

"Hold onto the sides, don't fall out of the boat
We really can't swim; we really can't float!"

Now Jack knew what Maggie was saying to him
Was really the truth; she and he could not swim.

No one had taught them to swim in the bay
Why, they swam not in water, but only in hay.

So, they held on tight to that boat and each other
Wishing they were at home with their father and mother.

They realized right there, in that small wooden shoe
That a farm on a hill could be really nice too.

They held on and waited for what seemed like a year,
Their arms held each other to keep out their fear.

Then the sea calmed down, their shoe started to float
Right back to land came that little boat.

They happily walked back to their little farm
Thankful to be safe and away from all harm.

Said Maggie to Jack, "that was a disaster
I have bumps and bruises, I need a plaster

To put on my head, then it won't ache so
I really hurt from my head to my toe!"

Then Jack looked at Maggie and he said to her,
"What went wrong with that trip, I'm not really sure

We made all out plans; we did what we should
It should not have been bad; it should have been good".

They thought and thought just what it could be
That made them so sad with their trip to the sea.

When they finally reached home, what a wonderful sight
The light from within was burning real bright.

Mom and Dad were awaiting that unhappy crew
The two little sailors from one wooden shoe.

"We missed you both; we're so glad you came home
We're been waiting here; we felt so alone".

Then they all gave kisses and hugs to each other
The mother, the father, the sister and brother.

Maggie and Jack, finally safe in their arms
Decided to stay and live on that farm.

A trip may be fun to go on some day
But for now they'll remain here to play in the hay.

After all they now know, wherever they roam
They both will agree; there is no place like home!

Acknowledgement

Thank you to my family for believing in my ability to give words a little of my imagination. Jim, I would like to say "thank you" for all your support in letting me know I am capable of creating memories that can be treasured forever. Jamie, McMurphy, Jen, Heidi, Erin, Mandy, Sean and Tim, the push that I needed to take that first step only happened through your belief in me. Kayla, Haley, Cody, Lissi, Tori, Jack and Maggie, thank you for letting me remember why children are children. Lisa, my dedicated editor, "thank you" to you and Dave for lending me your two imps for a lesson in life that hopefully we will all eventually learn. My dear friend Madeline, you plant a tree and only grow positive thoughts, thanks for the lesson. Jack and Maggie, just remember that your heart will always know where your true home is.

Dedication

This book is dedicated to Jack and Maggie. Maggie will always see life in a rainbow of colors and breathe the scent of the flowers that fill the air with the promise of happiness. Jack will always know that life is set in stories that define where he is going and who he will meet upon that road. May they always set their sights on great adventures, and let them forever remember that the greatest quest in life is to live in the love of one's family and never forget the place they first called home.